BOOK CLUB EDITION

IAN FLEMING'S

Story of
Chitty Chitty Bang Bang!
THE MAGICAL CAR

ADAPTED FOR BEGINNING READERS

By Al Perkins

Illustrated by B TOBEY –

BEGINNER BOOKS   A Division of Random House, Inc.

F G H 2

Jeremy Pott and his sister, Jemima,
were in the kitchen.
Mrs. Pott was making sandwiches.
They heard a noise outside.
They ran out to see what it was.

The noise came from
a great big car.
Mr. Pott was sitting in it.

GEN 11

"I found it in a junkyard,"
said Mr. Pott. "Jump in!

I'll take you all for a ride."

There were all kinds of lights
and buttons in the car.
Mr. Pott pushed the starter.
The engine made a noise.
It sounded like
"Chitty Chitty Bang Bang!"

"That's what we'll name our car,"
said Jeremy. "We'll call her
Chitty Chitty Bang Bang."

Mr. Pott drove out onto the highway.
Soon Chitty Chitty Bang Bang
was going a hundred miles an hour.

"Where are we going?" asked Mrs. Pott.

"To the beach," said Mr. Pott.

"We'll have a picnic."

But everyone else was going to the
beach too. Mr. Pott had to stop.
"This is not a good place
for a picnic," said Mrs. Pott.
"We'll just have to sit and wait,"
said Mr. Pott.

Then a button lighted up!
There were words on the button.

"Push it and see what happens,"
said Jeremy.
Mr. Pott pushed the button.

The engine made a humming noise.

The car began to shake.

Then wings came out.

Just like wings on an airplane!

"It's magic!" Jemima shouted.

"I guess it is magic," said Mr. Pott.
Chitty Chitty Bang Bang
flew up off the highway.

She flew over all the cars in front.

She flew up into the sky like a bird.

She headed for the beach.

Chitty Chitty Bang Bang
flew over the beach.
It was full of people.
"Where will we have our picnic?"
asked Mrs. Pott.
"There's no place to land."

Just then the steering wheel turned
in Mr. Pott's hands.
The car began to steer herself!

Chitty Chitty Bang Bang
flew away from the beach.
She flew out over the water.
She left the land far behind.

Then she pointed her nose down.

She dove straight toward the waves.

"We're going to crash!" said Mrs. Pott.

"We'll have a wet picnic."

But Chitty Chitty Bang Bang
didn't crash.
She pulled in her wings.
She landed on the water.

She headed for the beach.

"This must be France," said Jeremy.

"See the French flag

on the lighthouse."

"There's no one here," said Mrs. Pott.

"It's a fine place for a picnic."

She took out the picnic things.

She spread a tablecloth on the sand.

"Here's a big cave we can explore!"
cried Jeremy.

He and Jemima ran into the cave.

It looked dark and spooky inside.

"Look!" yelled Jemima.

There, just ahead, was a skeleton.

It swung back and forth.

Its bones rattled in the cold wind.

Jemima screamed.

24

Mr. and Mrs. Pott heard that scream.
They drove Chitty Chitty Bang Bang
into the cave.

"That's not a real skeleton,"
said Mr. Pott. "It's only a dummy."
Someone put it here to scare us.
Someone doesn't want us in this cave.
But we'll go in anyway."

They drove deeper and deeper
into the dark, gloomy cave.
Bats flew around their heads.

Water dripped from the rocks.

Spiders and snakes came out.

"What's that up ahead?" cried Jeremy.

It was a big room.

It was full of guns.

There were boxes of bombs and
barrels of gunpowder.

"This is strange," said Mr. Pott.

They saw a sign.

It was nailed to the wall.

They walked over and read it.

DANGER!
THESE GUNS BELONG TO Joe the Monster
HANDS OFF!!

"I know all about Joe the Monster,"
said Jeremy. "I read about him
in the paper. He's a bank robber!"
"This must be his secret cave,"
said Jemima.

33

"Let's blow up all this stuff,"
said Jeremy.

"That's a fine idea," said Mrs. Pott.

"Then we can have our picnic."

Mr. Pott put one end of a fuse
into a barrel of gunpowder.
He lighted the other end.
Then he said,
"Let's get out of here—fast!"

They got out just in time.

Boom! Boom!

The whole cave blew up.

Just then a big, black car drove up.

Three men jumped out.

They pointed guns at the Pott family.

"Hands up!" shouted one of the men.

"That's Joe the Monster!" said Jeremy.
"I've seen his picture in the paper."

"Tie up the two big ones,"
said Joe the Monster.
His men tied up Mr. and Mrs. Pott.
They tied them up tight.

Joe pushed Jemima and Jeremy
into the big, black car.
"We'll take these kids to Paris,"
he said. "We'll hold them for ransom."

Mr. and Mrs. Pott sat up.
They couldn't untie their hands.
They watched the
big, black car drive away.

Jeremy and Jemima looked out
of the big, black car.
Jemima began to cry.
"We'll never see Mother and Father
again!" she cried.

Then Chitty Chitty Bang Bang coughed.
She shook all over.
Then she made a humming noise.

Then she picked up Mrs. Pott.
She put her into the seat.
Then she picked up Mr. Pott.

Then Chitty Chitty Bang Bang
took the road to Paris.
Mr. and Mrs. Pott still had
their hands tied.

But Chitty Chitty Bang Bang
steered herself! She raced along
at one hundred miles an hour.
She raced after Joe the Monster
and the big, black car.

PARIS

They got closer and closer to Paris.
They got closer and closer
to the big, black car.

The two cars raced through Paris.
Chitty Chitty Bang Bang came
right up behind the big, black car.
She bit the big, black car!

Joe the Monster and his men
jumped out.
They ran upstairs into a house.

Jeremy and Jemima ran over to
Chitty Chitty Bang Bang.
Jeremy untied Mr. Pott.
Jemima untied Mrs. Pott.

Joe the Monster began shooting.
But Chitty Chitty Bang Bang
was not afraid of bullets.
She roared up the stairs.
Mr. Pott and Jeremy ran up behind her.

"I'm going to call
the police,"
said Mrs. Pott.

Chitty Chitty Bang Bang
went through the door.
She raced across the room.
She pushed Joe the Monster and
his men against the wall.

She pushed them so hard
they dropped their guns.
She held them until
the police got there.

The police put handcuffs
on Joe and his men.
They tied them all together.
They took them away to jail.

Then the chief of police
thanked the Pott family.
"You caught Joe for us," he said.
"Now, what can we do for you?"

"Please find us a place
to have our picnic," said Mrs. Pott.
"I am getting very hungry!"

The chief of police took them
to a beautiful park.
They all sat down to eat.
"I hope you like peanut butter,"
Mrs. Pott said to the chief of police.

Chitty Chitty Bang Bang ate too.

The French police fed her gasoline.

They fed her water.

They washed her and polished her
until she looked like new.

That night the Pott family
and Chitty Chitty Bang Bang
started back home.

"It will be nice to get home again,"
said Jemima.

"It sure will, said Jeremy. "But who knows
what will happen before we get there?"

A Special Offer for members of The Beginning Readers' Program ... Cat in the Hat Bookplates! Your child can personalize his or her books with these big (3″ by 4″) full color nameplates, available to members exclusively. Shipped 25 to the set for just $2.00, which *includes* shipping and handling! (New York and Connecticut residents must add state sales tax.) To order, simply send your name and complete address — remember your zip code — to the address below. Indicate the number of sets of 25 you wish. (These exclusive bookplates make wonderful fun gifts.) Allow 3-4 weeks for delivery.

The Beginning Readers' Program

A DIVISION OF GROLIER ENTERPRISES INC.
SHERMAN TURNPIKE, DANBURY, CT 06816